THE
SHERLOCK HOLMES

CHILDREN'S COLLECTION

CREATURES, CODES AND CURIOUS CASES

Published by Sweet Cherry Publishing Limited
Unit 36, Vulcan House,
Vulcan Road,
Leicester, LE5 3EF
United Kingdom

First published in the UK in 2021
2021 edition

2 4 6 8 10 9 7 5 3 1

ISBN: 978-1-78226-431-6

© Sweet Cherry Publishing

Sherlock Holmes: The Empty House

Cover design by Arianna Bellucci and Amy Booth
Illustrations by Arianna Bellucci

Lexile® code numerical measure L = Lexile® 720L

Guided Reading Level = W

www.sweetcherrypublishing.com

Printed and bound in India
I.TP002

SHERLOCK HOLMES

THE EMPTY HOUSE

SIR ARTHUR CONAN DOYLE

Chapter One

It had been three years since
my friend, Sherlock Holmes,
disappeared over the Reichenbach
Falls in Switzerland along with his
enemy, Moriarty.

I shall always remember
that dreadful day. I had been
tricked into going back to the
hotel, leaving Holmes alone and

in danger. By the time I had returned to the waterfall, the fatal fight was over. All that was left were the few items Holmes had meant for me to find: his walking stick, his cigarette case and a note. The words are etched on my brain.

My dear Watson,

Professor Moriarty has been kind enough to let me write these few lines. He is waiting until I am finished for us to discuss the problems that lie between us.

... my career has, in any case, reached its end. And no possible ending could be any better than this. I was quite sure that the letter calling you back to the hotel was a trick. I let you leave knowing that something like this would follow ...

I still missed him very much. There wasn't a corner of London that did not remind me of him.

I once thought I saw him. I had been walking home from visiting a patient and as I turned onto

7

Regent Street I saw the shadow of a man cast on the wall. It was a tall, thin figure with a hawk-like face. I was so sure it was Holmes. I almost cried out to him, but then the man stepped out into the light and I could see that, of course, it wasn't him. I felt like a fool. I needed to face the truth.

My friend, Sherlock Holmes, had gone forever.

Chapter Two

I still took an interest in police investigations, and I often came across cases that I knew Holmes would have loved to solve. I sometimes found myself thinking of the list of his talents I had written when I was first getting to know him. I tried to mimic those skills to unravel the cases, but I would never be as good as him.

Sherlock Holmes

Knowledge

- Chemistry — extensive. Does a lot of experiments
- An expert on plant-based poisons but ignorant of gardening
- Can tell different soils and muds from one another
- Expert boxer and swordsman
- Knows a lot about human and animal anatomy
- Expert in British law and criminal history — knows every detail of every horror committed this century
- Plays violin well
- Can tell the difference between types of tobacco
- Can identify a perfume by one sniff

Nevertheless, I was trying. I was becoming more and more observant, and was even able to tell the difference between some types of tobacco. I thought that having a knowledge of rare poisons would be useful too, especially since I already knew a little about it, being a doctor. So I studied the topic daily. I was also rereading many of my reports of Sherlock's old cases – I was finally starting to see how he went about solving them.

Then came the murder of Mr Ronald Adair in March 1894. The whole of London was shocked at his death. He was very well liked and didn't seem to have an enemy in the world.

According to the reports, on the night of his death, he arrived back home at ten o'clock. His mother and sister were out. The maid had lit a fire in his sitting room and there was a lot of smoke, so she had opened a window. She heard him arrive home and go into his room.

Later, at around eleven-thirty, his mother and sister arrived home. They went to say goodnight to Mr Adair, but the door was locked from the inside. They were so worried when he did not answer that they asked their neighbour to break the door down.

Poor Mr Adair was lying on the floor, dead. He had been shot, but there was no sign of a gun. There was money on the table – thirty-seven pounds. It was arranged in little piles as though he had been counting it, and next to it sat a sheet of paper with names on.

Everyone seemed to have their own theory about what happened, but most made no sense. No one could answer the most important question: how did the

murderer get in and out? The window was six metres from the ground. There were no drainpipes to climb up, and the flower bed beneath had not been trampled.

And why was the door locked on the inside? Had the murderer hidden in the room while Mr Adair's mother and sister discovered the crime, and then escaped later? Even if he had, that didn't answer the question of how he got in there in the first place.

And how was he not seen? Park Lane is a busy road, even so late at night. Surely, when the criminal did manage to conduct an escape, he would have been seen by *someone*.

It was a mystery indeed. A mystery I was determined to solve.

The morning after the murder, I read every newspaper article written about it.

The Honourable
Robert Adair, son of
the Earl of Maynooth,
was found dead late
last night by his
mother and sister.

The door was locked from the
inside but the window was left
open. What could have been the
motive? There was money on the
table, so it wasn't a burglary.

Yet death came in a most strange
form for this young aristocrat.

THE HONOURABLE ROBERT ADAIR SHOT DEAD AT HIS HOME IN PARK LANE

The victim had formerly been engaged to Miss Edith Woodley, of Carstairs. It is thought that the decision to break up was mutual, and that they remained friends.

RICH BACHELOR SHOT DEAD AFTER WINNING AT CARDS

The Earl of Maynooth's son, Robert Adair, was shot last night at his mansion in Park Lane. He had spent the evening gambling at one of the many clubs he belonged to, and a large amount of his winnings were still on the table. His door was locked from the inside and his window left open. Was this an act of revenge or jealousy?

None of them could offer a plausible answer.

All day, on my rounds, I continued churning over the facts, looking for new clues that other people had not spotted yet. But I simply had no idea how the criminal had done it, let alone who that criminal was.

I wished that Holmes were there. How he would have loved this mystery! I realised more than ever what the public had lost with his death.

Chapter Three

After visiting my last patient of
the day, I happened to find myself
near Hyde Park and the scene of
the crime. I crossed the park, so
focussed on where I was going
that I almost forgot to admire the
newly-flowering tulips. Soon I
arrived at the end of Park Lane. A
group of people were standing on

the pavement looking up at the window of a house. I guessed that was where Mr Adair had died.

There was a little scuffle as the crowd moved in to hear a tall, thin man – whom I assumed was

a plain-clothed detective – giving his theories on what he thought had happened. His ideas seemed ridiculous. He said the murderer could be an acrobat from the local circus, who had scaled the wall to get in and out of the house.

'Or maybe it was a rock climber,' he bellowed to the crowd. Whispers buzzed through the crowd like a swarm of flies.

'Was Adair a spy, or a member of a high-class gang who had to be assassinated?' More whispers, more buzzing. 'Perhaps someone has invented a silent gun that can be shot without anyone seeing or hearing it.'

I stepped back in frustration. How I missed my friend at this moment. I knew he could have solved the case far quicker than any policeman.

As I backed away, I almost knocked over the old man who was standing behind me. He dropped the pile of heavy books that he had been carrying, scattering them across the pavement. I bent down to help him pick them up. One of them was called *The Origin of Tree*

Worship. What an unusual title! *He must be a collector of rare books*, I thought, feeling even more guilty as I brushed some dirt off one of them.

I apologised, but he waved his hand angrily and hobbled away, gripping the books tightly to his chest.

I turned my attention back to the scene of the crime. In front of Mr Adair's house was a low wall and a railing less than two metres high. It would be easy to get into the garden but there was no way anyone could climb up to the window or down again without a rope. I tried to think like Holmes. 'Always begin with the most obvious answer first,' he would say. But that didn't help. There was no obvious answer.

I made my way home as puzzled as ever. I reached my study and was just about to delve into one of Holmes' old notebooks when the maid knocked on my door.

'Mr Watson, sir, you have a visitor.' To my surprise, it was the old man whose books I had knocked to the ground.

His sharp, lined face peered out from a frame of white hair. He was dressed in tatty trousers and his frock-coat was too big. He was still carrying about a dozen books under his right arm.

29

'You're surprised to see me, sir,' he said in a strange, croaky voice. 'I just thought I'd apologise for being so gruff earlier. Thank you for picking up my books.'

'It was nothing,' I said. 'There was no need for you to come all this way just to apologise. How did you know where I lived?'

He ignored the question. 'I have a couple of books here that would fill that gap in your bookshelf rather neatly,' he said, pointing behind me.

I turned to look at the bookshelf, and when I turned back again Mr Sherlock Holmes was standing in front of me, smiling.

My head swam. A grey mist swirled in front of my eyes and suddenly everything went black.

Chapter Four

I woke up sitting in my chair. Holmes was standing over me, waving smelling salts under my nose.

'My dear Watson,' he said in his familiar voice. 'I'm sorry I made you faint. A thousand apologies. I had no idea that would happen.'

I gripped his arm. 'Holmes! Is it really you?' This was my wishful thinking at work again. Now both my eyes and my ears were deceiving me. Was I losing my mind?

But the face in front of me did not change shape or disappear. It *was* real. He nodded and smiled broadly.

I shook my head. 'I often think I see you. Just the other night … Have I entirely lost my senses?'

'You always were over-imaginative, Watson, but this time you can believe your eyes and ears. It really is me.'

Holmes leaned back, pulled out his pipe from his pocket and lit it.

He was still dressed in the old clothes, but the white hair and

the books were on the table. He
looked thinner than he used to be,
and his face was pale.

'But, how did you climb out of
that abyss under the waterfall?
Even you are not superhuman.'

'Oh, do not worry about that,
Watson. Are *you* all right? I gave
you a great shock just now.'

'I am fine,' I said. 'But I can
hardly believe my eyes.' I gripped
his arm again. 'You are real. You
aren't a ghost. Please tell me how

you escaped from that deadly
waterfall.'

'Not now, my dear fellow,' he
said. 'I have some dangerous work
to do tonight and I need your help.
It will be just like the old days. We
shall have time for dinner before
we go. I will tell you about my
escape when all of this is over.'

'Oh, no. I want to hear it now,'
I said.

Holmes raised his eyebrow at
me. 'Well, if you insist … I had no

trouble getting out of it because I was never in it.'

'You were never in it?'

'No, Watson. I saw Moriarty standing on the path blocking my way. There was a look of triumph in his eyes. He knew he had me cornered. I asked him if I could write you a note and he said yes.

My dear Watson,

Professor Moriarty has been kind enough to let me write these few lines. He is waiting until I am finished for us to discuss the problems that lie between us.
He has been telling me how he

As you know, I left it on the rock with my cigarette case and my walking stick.

'Then Moriarty rushed at me. He knew this was the end of his criminal career, and he wanted

revenge. If it was the last thing he did, he would take me with him into that dreadful hole. We tottered at the edge of the falls and his long arms were around me.'

Holmes smiled and his eyes glinted with amusement. It was an expression so familiar to me that I smiled back.

'I thought it was the end for me too. The rocks under my feet were slippery from the spray. The water roared past my ears and I was prepared to go to my death and take that evil man with me.

'But just for a moment I had an advantage. I could feel that he was slightly off balance, yet my feet were secure. I have some knowledge of Bartitsu, the Japanese martial art, so I twisted out of his grip and was free. Moriarty staggered and clawed at the air with his hands, desperately trying to grip onto something. But he could not regain his balance and with a deafening scream, he fell. I watched him fall a long way before I heard him splash into the water far below.'

I could barely believe it.

'But the tracks!' I cried. 'Two sets of footprints went down the path and none returned.'

Holmes nodded. 'Ah, yes. I did think of walking backwards down the path, so it wouldn't look like anyone had come back, but I knew you would see through that trick.'

I was flattered that he should think my deduction skills were so good.

'You see, Watson, I realised what a great chance I had to let people think I was dead. Then Moriarty's gang would be careless, and I could track them down and destroy them in secret.'

'But if you didn't walk back down the path, how did you

escape? There was
nothing but a sheer wall
behind you.'

'Actually, the wall was
not quite sheer,' he said.
'Though I know that is
what you claimed in the
report you wrote in
the newspaper. There
were a few footholds.
It was not an easy
climb. One mistake
would have been

fatal. Several times the tufts of grass I clung to came away in my hand or my foot slipped on the wet rock. But at last I reached a small ledge and rested, thinking I was safe.

'Then something unexpected happened. A huge rock roared past me, bounced off the path and hurled into the water below. I thought it was an accident, until I looked up and saw a man's head silhouetted against the sky.

One of Moriarty's gang had come with him. He must have seen his friend's death and my escape. Now he was trying to do what Moriarty had failed to.

'Shakily, I pushed myself up onto my feet and flattened my body against the side of the cliff. This meant there was no way he could aim another killer rock in my direction. I stood there, my hands gripping the cool stone behind me for what felt like an eternity. Finally, I braved myself to have another look up at where the man had stood, but he was gone. I had escaped for now, but he knew I was still alive. I was still in danger.

'I was working through plan after plan in my head of what to do next, when something below caught my eye. It was you, Watson. I watched as you walked along the track: as you found my walking stick and my letter and

as you realised what must have
happened. I could see your grief
and I almost called out.'

'I would have kept your secret,' I
said, feeling a little hurt.

'I know you would have tried
to. Several times I almost wrote
to you, but I knew that it would
be difficult for you to keep up
the pretence. The only person
I told was my brother, Mycroft,
who sent me money to live on.
Moriarty's man knew I was

still alive, so I had to disappear completely.'

'Where did you go?'

'Once I had made my way off the cliff, I ran as far away as I could. I must have travelled ten miles over the mountains that night. Luckily, there was a full moon to light my way. I fell a couple

48

of times but kept going, knowing that Moriarty's man might be following. Eventually, with my clothes in tatters and my shoes barely clinging to my weary feet, I crossed the border into Italy and went to Florence.

'After recovering in that beautiful city, I travelled for two years in Tibet and spent some time with the Dalai Llama. Then I went to Mecca and Khartoum before coming back to Europe. Did you hear about the adventures of the Norwegian explorer, Sigerson?'

I nodded, puzzled. I had spent many evenings sitting by the fire, reading about that man's travels.

Holmes smiled. 'But you didn't suspect for one moment that it was your friend, did you?'

I laughed. 'Holmes!'

'After that I went to France and worked in a laboratory doing

experiments,' he went on, 'until
I heard the news that one of
Moriarty's remaining men had
died. I knew that two of his gang
had never been caught. While
both had roamed the streets
of London, it was too risky to
return, but now there was only
one left. I could deal with him.
I was already thinking about
coming back when I heard about
this Park Lane mystery and the
murder of Mr Ronald Adair.

The case intrigued me so much that I couldn't resist returning to London. So I packed my bags, hopped on the next train and went straight to my old rooms in Baker Street.'

'But Mrs Hudson ...' I began.

Holmes laughed. 'She didn't quite faint as you did, Watson. She slammed the door in my face, thinking I was a ghost. It took a little persuasion for her to open it again. Then she flung her arms around me and became quite hysterical. Not like our calm Mrs Hudson at all.'

'She is very fond of you, Holmes. I saw her once or twice after you disappeared and she mourned you for a long time.'

'Yes, she was rather overdramatic, but I dare say she has been learning from the best.' He smirked at me, waiting for a reaction, but I resisted.

'Well, there is work for us tonight, Watson,' he said. 'After that we can catch up on the last three years.'

I looked at his keen face. But it suddenly transformed from looking excited to looking almost sad. Holmes put his hand on my arm. 'I heard about your wife, my dear Watson. I cannot imagine your sadness at losing her after so short a time together.'

I could see his eyes glistening with tears. It brought back the terrible grief I had suffered a

year ago when my sweet Mary died. First I had lost my friend and then my sweetheart. There was nothing I could do for either. Maybe one day they will find a cure for tuberculosis, but it was too late for dear Mary.

'Work is the best antidote to sorrow,' Holmes said, pulling my mind back into the room. 'And I have a piece of work for us tonight that is most important.'

Chapter Five

At nine o'clock that evening we climbed into a hansom cab. I had my friend by my side and the thrill of adventure in my heart. Holmes was cold, stern and silent. As we passed a street lamp I could see that his brows were knotted together in thought. What wild beast were we about to hunt down in the dark jungle of criminal London?

Holmes stopped the cab at the corner of Cavendish Square. We got out and he looked around to make sure no one was about. Then he led me through a maze of alleyways that I never knew existed, until we reached a narrow lane lined with gloomy houses. Keeping to the shadows, Holmes and I made our way down the lane, through a wooden

gate, and into a deserted garden.

Holmes reached into his pocket
for a key and opened the back door
of a house. We stepped in together.

It was pitch-black and clearly
empty. Our feet creaked over
the wooden floorboards. As
I felt my way along the wall,
pieces of damp wallpaper
peeled off in my hands.
Holmes' cold, thin
fingers closed around
my wrist. He led

me down a long hall and into a large, square room, closing the door behind us. A dim light came in through the window from the gaslamps in the street. Against one wall stood an old wooden bookcase.

I could just see the shape of Holmes. He put his hand on my shoulders and whispered in my ear.

'Do you know where we are?'

'Surely that is Baker Street?' I said, peering through the window.

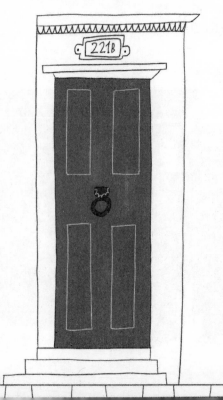

'Correct. We are in Camden House, directly opposite our own apartment.'

'But why are we here?' I asked.

'Because it gives an excellent view of Number 221B,' he said. 'Watson, please go a little closer to the window, but make sure nobody can see you. Then look up at our old rooms.'

I crept forwards and looked across at the familiar window. I gasped. The blind was down and

there was a strong light in the
window. I could clearly see the
shadow of a man behind the blind.

The poise of the head and the
shape of the shoulders were so

familiar. It was a perfect replica
of Holmes! I reached out to make
sure the man himself was really
here beside me. He was shaking
with silent laughter.

'Well?' he said.

'Good heavens!' I cried. 'It's marvellous!'

'It is rather like me, isn't it?'

'I would swear that it was you.'

'When I was in France, I had a waxwork sculpture of myself made. This afternoon I arranged it by the window.'

Waxworks

Made from solid wax, waxworks are made to represent famous people, to remember those who have passed away, or for those cunning enough to use them as a decoy. If crafted by a talented sculptor, a waxwork could deceive others into thinking you are somewhere when you are not.

'But why?'

'Because, dear Watson, I want certain people to think that I am there, back in my rooms.'

'You think the rooms are being watched?'

'I *know* they are,' he said.

'By whom?'

'By my old enemies. The last member of Moriarty's gang is the man who tried to kill me at Reichenbach Falls. I saw one of his servants watching the place.

The servant is harmless, but his boss was a close friend of Moriarty's and is now the most dangerous man in London. That is the man who is after me tonight.'

I could now see what my friend's plans were. The watchers were being watched and the trackers tracked. The silhouette of Holmes in the window was the bait, and we were the hunters. We were leading the criminals straight to us!

We stood together in darkness. Holmes was silent and still, but I knew he was alert, watching everyone who passed by in the street.

It was a bleak night and the wind whistled shrilly down the long road. People were muffled in their coats and scarves.

I noticed two men sheltering in a doorway up the street. I tried to point them out to Holmes, but he just gave a grunt of impatience. Perhaps they were nothing to do with this plan, but they certainly looked suspicious. A few minutes passed and I saw Holmes glance at the men once or twice. Then he began to tap his fingers on the wall and shuffle his feet about.

As midnight grew nearer there were fewer people in the street. Holmes was now pacing up and down in a very agitated way.

Suddenly, I grabbed his arm and pointed across the street to the window. 'The shadow has moved!'

Instead of the side of its face, we could now see the back of the head.

'Of course it has moved!' cried Holmes. 'I'm not stupid enough to leave it in one position. Do you think that would fool some of the sharpest men in Europe? We have been in this room for two hours. Dear Mrs Hudson has moved the statue eight times – once every fifteen minutes.'

I blushed. I hadn't noticed it at all. I was also a little worried about Mrs Hudson's safety. What if she got shot while moving the wax statue? Holmes must have been desperate.

'Ah!' he cried. He took a quick, excited breath.

Outside, the street was empty. All was still and dark except for the lit window of 221B.

Again he made an excited hissing sound. Then he pulled me into the darkest corner of the room and put his finger against my lips. I could feel the finger shaking.

Chapter Six

The dark street still looked empty.

Then I heard it. A low
shuffling sound came from
behind us – from the very house
we were in! A door opened
and closed. Steps crept down
the passage. Each creaking
floorboard told us that the
person was getting closer.

Holmes crouched back against the wall in the corner, next to the half-broken bookcase, and I did the same.

I'm sure Holmes had not anticipated his enemy following us into the house. Had he followed us all the way here? If so, why had he taken so long to enter the house?

The floorboards continued to creak in a regular pattern, the sound echoing around the empty house. The footsteps finally stopped directly outside the door. There was a small squeak as the doorknob turned.

I saw the dim shape of a man in the doorway. He stood for a moment and then crept forwards into the room, only a couple of metres from us.

I held my breath, expecting him to see us any moment, but he did not. He crept softly to the window and opened it a few

centimetres. He kneeled down and looked through the gap.
A street lamp shone onto his excited face. His eyes glowed like a fire in the dark room.

He was an older man with a long, thin nose and a bushy moustache that was peppered with grey. His face was slim and angular, with deep lines.

He carried what looked like a stick, but as he laid it on the floor a metallic clang rang around the

room. My stomach dropped. This
was not a stick, but some kind
of gun.

The man busied himself
pulling, pushing and
twisting different parts of
the gun into place, before a
sudden loud click. He bent
forwards and pushed a
lever. There was a long,
whirling, grinding noise
and another click.

Holmes didn't move a

muscle, and I knew that, like me, he didn't dare to breathe.

The man stood up and rested the gun's barrel on the windowsill.

I saw his moustache droop over the gun and his eye gleam as he peered along the sights. His target was the wax model in the window across the street. I shuddered to think that it could really have been Holmes. He often stood at the window, especially when he was thinking.

The man gave a sigh of satisfaction and then his finger tightened on the trigger.

There was a strange, loud whizz and the tinkle of broken glass.

At that moment Holmes sprang like a tiger onto the man's back and they crashed to the floor. We had the element of surprise on our side but as I watched, the man escaped my friend's clutches and headed for the door. I leaped forwards and grabbed the man by his wrist

to pull him back into the room,
but he was too strong. He swung
his arm to the side and sent me
crashing into the wall. Holmes ran
at the man, anger burning behind
his eyes. He wrestled him to the

ground and managed to pin one of his arms down before the other flew through the air and straight into his jaw. Holmes yelped but did not let go of the criminal.

'Watson,' he gasped, 'find me something to restrain this villain.'

I scanned the room in panic and saw an old bell-pull hanging from the wall. I tore it from its rusted fixtures and passed it to Holmes. He tied the man's hands together and asked me to hold him so that he could not escape.

Then Holmes sprang to his feet, leaned out of the window and blew hard on a whistle he had taken from his pocket. In a moment there was the clatter

of running feet along the corridor behind us. Two policemen and a plain-clothed detective rushed in through the door.

'Is that you, Lestrade?' asked Holmes.

Inspector Lestrade paused in the doorway. 'Yes, Mr Holmes. So it really is you! I could hardly believe it when they told me at the station that you were still alive. It's good to see you back in London, sir.'

'I thought you needed a little help,' said Holmes. 'Three unsolved murders in one year is not good, Lestrade. And your hiding place in the street this evening was not much better. Huddling in a doorway? Watson saw you the instant we looked outside.'

The inspector grunted and looked down. He could not deny that Holmes was speaking the truth.

We all stood up. The prisoner was now on his feet, breathing hard and being held on each side by a policeman.

A few people had seen the police rush into the house and had gathered in the street to see what was going on. Holmes closed the window and the blind. Then the policemen lit their lamps.

I was able to have a good look at the prisoner.

He had cruel blue eyes and he stared fiercely at Holmes. 'You clever, clever fiend,' he muttered.

'Ah, Colonel,' said Holmes. 'I don't think I've had the pleasure of seeing you since you hurled rocks at me at the Reichenbach Falls. I have not introduced you yet.'

Holmes looked round at us all.

'Gentlemen, this is Colonel Sebastian Moran. He is the best shot in the Indian Army. He was a legend in his regiment. They say that he could hit a moving target from fifty metres away.'

The fierce man said nothing, but glared at my companion. His eyes were savage and his

moustache bristled like the fur of
an angry cat.

'I'm surprised that my simple
trick could fool you,' said Holmes,
teasingly. 'You could not tell a
wax replica from the real me?
Tut, tut.'

Colonel Moran sprang
forwards with a
snarl
of rage,
but the
policemen

dragged him back again. The
fury on his face was terrible to
look at.

'You surprised me too,' said
Holmes. 'I didn't expect you to
use this house. I thought you
would shoot from the street
where my friend, Lestrade, and
his men were waiting.'

Holmes picked up the gun from
the floor. He looked at it closely.

'A good choice of weapon,' he
said. 'It's silent and powerful.

I knew that Moriarty had it made specially for you, Colonel, but I had never seen it.

'See how it can be mistaken for a walking stick, Watson? You could walk around London with it and no one would suspect a thing.

He then turned to Lestrade. 'What are you going to charge him with?'

Lestrade looked surprised. 'The attempted murder of Mr Sherlock Holmes, of course.'

Holmes shook his head. 'No, Lestrade. Keep me out of it. You must have the credit for his arrest. With your usual cunning and courage you have got him. Congratulations!'

'Got whom, Mr Holmes?'

'The man who shot Mr Ronald Adair in Park Lane last month. The man the whole police force has been looking for.'

Chapter Seven

The prisoner was taken away
and Holmes and I went across
the road to our old rooms. I was
amazed that they had been left
unchanged for the three years
that Holmes had been away. His
brother Mycroft and Mrs Hudson
had seen to that.

As we went in, I looked around.

There was the acid-stained table where Holmes carried out his chemical experiments. And there was the shelf of scrapbooks and reference books.

The violin case lay on a chair, the pipe rack on the wall, and even the Persian slippers containing his tobacco were where they had always been.

There were two people in the room. Mrs Hudson, who beamed at us both, and the strange dummy that had played such an important part in the evening's adventures.

'What a mess, Mr Holmes, what a mess! But I'm glad to see that it was worth it.'

'I hope you were very careful, Mrs Hudson,' said Holmes.

'I went to it on my knees, Mr Holmes, just as you said.'

'Did you see where the bullet went?'

She reached into her pocket. 'It went right through the statue, then hit the wall and fell onto the carpet. Here it is, sir.'

Holmes passed it to me. 'A revolver bullet. Who would imagine that such a large bullet could be fired from an airgun?'

But I was not thinking of that. I was holding the piece of lead that could have been the end of

Holmes. Such a small thing could have marked the end of such a great man.

Mrs Hudson left and we settled down in our old chairs. Holmes reached for his pipe and lit it.

'Hand me the book of biographies please, Watson,' he said.

I did so.

'My collection of M's is a fine one, but here. Read this.'

He handed me the book.

The second most dangerous man in London.

MORAN, Sebastian, Colonel. Born London 1840. Educated in Eton and Oxford. Formerly 1st Bengalore Pioneers. Served in several campaigns. Author of several books on Indian wildlife.

In the margin Holmes had written, "The second most dangerous man in London".

I handed the book back to Holmes. 'He was an honourable soldier.'

'It is true. Up to a point he did well. He was a very brave man, but somewhere along the way he went wrong. He came back to London and met Moriarty, who gave him some criminal jobs to do that no others would try.

'You may remember the death of Mrs Stewart in 1887? I'm sure that Colonel Moran was at the bottom of that, although nothing could be proved.

'And do you remember when I came to see you in your rooms three years ago, and asked that you close the shutters because I was afraid of airguns?'

I nodded.

'I knew of the existence of that gun and that one of the best shots in the world would be behind it. When we were in Switzerland, Colonel Moran followed us with Moriarty. He was the one who tried to kill me after Moriarty had failed.'

The whole thing was becoming clear to me now. I was amazed at how Holmes could keep one step ahead of these clever, evil men.

'I could not come back to London,' he went on. 'So I waited. Then, when I heard about the death of Mr Ronald Adair, I knew

that Colonel Moran had done it.
Now was my chance. He played
cards with Adair. He followed
him home and then shot him
through the open window. That's
why no one could work out how
the murderer got in and out of the
room – because he never did. He
shot Mr Adair from outside.

'I knew that this was the same
way Colonel Moran would try to
kill me. So I carefully lured him
with my silhouette in the window

and made sure that Inspector Lestrade and his men were hiding outside, ready to pounce. Though with their poor attempt at hiding, I'm surprised Colonel Moran didn't spot them himself.'

'But why did Colonel Moran kill Mr Adair?' I asked.

'I can only guess,' said Holmes. 'But I think that they had been partners in a card game and had won a large sum of money. Mr Adair had caught Colonel Moran cheating and had threatened to tell someone if Colonel Moran didn't resign from the card club. That would have ruined him – he lived off the money from his winnings.

'Mr Adair had the money out on his desk because he was working out how much money he should pay back to whom. He didn't want to keep the money he'd won by cheating.'

That seemed like a logical explanation. 'I have no doubt that you're right, Holmes.'

'And that unique gun,' said Holmes, stretching out in his

chair and crossing his legs, 'will be displayed in the Scotland Yard Museum.'

A broad smile stretched across his face. 'Once again Mr Sherlock Holmes is free to solve the many little mysteries of London.'

Sherlock Holmes

World-renowned private
detective Sherlock Holmes has
solved hundreds of mysteries,
and is the author of such
fascinating monographs as
Early English Charters and *The
Influence of a Trade Upon the Form of
a Hand.* He keeps bees in his free time.

Dr John Watson

Wounded in action at Maiwand,
Dr John Watson left the army and
moved into 221B Baker Street. There
he was surprised to learn that his
new friend, Sherlock Holmes, faced
daily peril solving crimes, and began
documenting his investigations.
Dr Watson also runs a doctor's practice.

To download Sherlock Holmes activities, please visit
www.sweetcherrypublishing.com/resources